8

Pepper's Quest

HarperCollins®, ☰®, and Harper Festival®
are trademarks of HarperCollins Publishers.

Bella Sara #8: Pepper's Quest
Cover and interior illustrations by Heather Theurer
Copyright © 2009 Hidden City Games, Inc. © 2005–2009 conceptcard. All rights reserved.
BELLA SARA is a trademark of conceptcard and is used by Hidden City Games under license.
Licensed by Granada Ventures Limited.
Printed in the United States of America.

Library of Congress catalog card number: 2009920769
ISBN 978-0-06-168787-7
❖
09 10 11 12 13   CG/CW   10 9 8 7 6 5 4 3
First Edition

Bella Sara™

8

Pepper's Quest

Written by Felicity Brown
Illustrated by Heather Theurer

HarperFestival®
A Division of HarperCollinsPublishers

A golden glitterbug swooped around Jillian Frouda's head, trailing tiny amber sparkles.

Jillian groaned. She was practicing her natural ability to call animals to her, and she'd been aiming to entice the pretty yellow daybats to approach. Instead she'd summoned another pesky glitterbug. Jillian waved her hand at the insect buzzing above her, shooing it away from her long, curly red hair. Glitterbug sparkles stained hair and took forever to wash out.

Behind her, Jillian heard snarling laughter. "Don't make fun of me, Conall," she said to her oldest friend. "I'm trying my best."

"You didn't summon a swarm this time," Conall replied. "You're improving."

Conall was a burly, charcoal-colored wolf who had been transformed so that he now had the legs of a horse. His voice was a deep growl that was difficult for anybody in Canter Hollow except Jillian to understand—but then nobody else had grown up in Styginmoor Castle among warrior wolves. The other wolves' snarling voices sounded evil, but Conall hadn't started to speak until after his transformation, and his growl was softer and more gentle.

"It would work better if you used your book," he said now.

Jillian shook her head. "I can't use my memory journal, Fuzzy Foot. It came from Ivenna, and it reminds me of all the nasty things she made me do with it. So

I have to learn to use my ability without it." Ivenna was the evil mistress of Styginmoor Castle, and she'd stolen Jillian as a baby away from her parents. As Jillian grew older, Ivenna had tricked her into calling magical animals to the castle so she could use their powers.

"I understand," Conall growled, sinking his haunches down beside Jillian. He shook his left front hoof awkwardly. "You should think of a new nickname for me. These new feet aren't fuzzy."

"I'm sorry," Jillian apologized. "You're getting better at walking on your new legs, though. You've been practicing, too."

Conall nodded. "Some things I'll never be able to do again," he said, sounding frustrated. "Right now, I'd be happy if I could just jump and run properly."

"We both have to practice more," Jillian replied. "It's the only way to feel like our real selves again."

After Conall wobbled off toward

the brook on the far edge of the cottage's yard, Jillian tried to gather her strength before calling the daybats again. The land around the cottage was lush, with an amazing variety of trees and plants that almost glowed in the late afternoon sunlight. The cottage was small but sweet, with cream-colored walls and a dark blue roof. It had been generous of the townspeople to let her stay there after she'd escaped to Canter Hollow. But it still didn't feel quite like home.

With a sigh, Jillian focused on the daybats. She closed her eyes and relaxed, gently coaxing them to fly to her side.

But her concentration was broken by familiar memories. A pair of sparkling green eyes peered down at her: her mother's eyes, shining with love at Jillian when she was a baby. In her mind she heard the sound of her father's deep, happy laughter, and she recalled the sturdy Travelers' caravan, decorated with yellow and turquoise swirls, that had been her home.

Jillian opened her eyes. The memories of her infancy were getting stronger lately, which made it difficult to focus on practicing her ability. The images also left her feeling lonely and incomplete, longing for the family and childhood she'd lost.

Maybe Canter Hollow doesn't feel like home because I never knew my real home, she thought.

But she couldn't let the memories keep sidetracking her. Tightening her hands into fists, Jillian returned her attention to the daybats and reached out with her mind, urging them to come to her.

Just as she felt a spark of connection with the daybats, it was broken by a different flash of memory: the beautiful Starstone Otter gazing up at her, looking terribly forlorn locked up in Ivenna's dark prison. Jillian shuddered as she recalled the horrid sound of Ivenna's mocking laughter—

The daybats, startled by the broken

connection, fluttered out of the tree. They swooped over the cottage, disappearing toward the setting sun.

Jillian decided that was a sign to give up practicing until tomorrow.

That night, Jillian had a vivid dream. She twitched uncomfortably in her sleep as she fell into a deep vision.

She stood in a wide, grassy meadow speckled with wildflowers. Flashing insects swarmed around her as the sound of hooves echoed across the field, heading her way.

Jillian's mouth dropped open as a horse leaped over a line of hedges and galloped across the field. The horse was a speckled roan, with a velvety blue-gray hide marked with hundreds of black flecks. His mane and tail flowed behind him like smoke.

Jillian wasn't afraid—she felt as though she'd known this horse her whole life. He slowed as he galloped past, and

Jillian leaped onto his back.

Together they rushed across the endless field. Jillian had never felt such pure joy, and as the horse bunched his muscles and jumped, soaring over a narrow stream, she knew they would be together their whole lives.

Jillian woke to the sound of morning birdsong outside the cottage, overwhelmed by the lingering dream of the speckled roan.

After getting dressed, Jillian grabbed some fruit from the kitchen and headed outside to find Conall. He was near his favorite spot by the brook, under a canopy of broad-leaved trees, practicing jumping. Jillian watched from a distance as he hopped on his shaky horse legs. He was still wobbling when he landed.

Jillian hurried over. "Good morning," she said, "and good jumping."

Conall rolled his eyes. "You're just being nice," he said. Then he hunkered down on a thick patch of grass and curled up his gangly legs. "I love it here. The water's clean, and the grass smells sweet."

"Nothing like Styginmoor," said Jillian.

"Nothing at all," Conall replied contentedly.

Jillian sat on a rock beside the brook. "I had a very strong dream," she said, and quickly filled him in on the details. "It felt so real. I just know this horse is out there somewhere. He's important. I'm supposed to meet him, I think."

"Call him to you," Conall suggested. "Dreams that powerful come to you for a reason."

Jillian dipped her foot into the brook. The water tingled against her toes. Under the surface, tiny red sea-horses danced around the bubbles trailing from her feet. As spots of light and shadow shifted on the water, Jillian realized that they reminded her of the markings on the speckled roan.

"I'll do it," she decided. She closed her eyes and let her memory of the dream wash over her. Images of shadowy horses raced past her inner vision in a foggy landscape. Then one horse solidified and turned toward her.

It was the speckled roan stallion. Seeing him again made Jillian's heart swell with happiness. *Come to me,* she called. *I know we are meant to be together.*

The stallion's dark eyes glowed as the connection between them sizzled with intense energy.

Jillian opened her eyes on the bank of the brook. Beside her, Conall was watching her alertly.

"It worked," Jillian said, leaning her shoulder against her friend's thick fur. "I think it did, anyway."

"Good," Conall growled. "Now you can stop whining about using your ability without the journal." He gave her a wolf grin to let her know he was joking.

"What happens now?"

"He'll take time to get here," Jillian replied. "Might as well finish breakfast." She took a bite of a pink plum.

After she'd eaten, Jillian and Conall headed back toward the cottage. Even though Jillian knew it was too soon for the roan to arrive, she still hoped he would already be in the front yard, waiting. But as they walked up the path, there was no horse in sight.

Jillian swallowed her disappointment. It was unreasonable to think that the roan could get there that quickly, no matter how much she wanted to meet him. She would just have to wait.

Then Conall stiffened beside her, sniffing the air.

Jillian heard a snort, and the roan stallion stepped around the corner of the cottage.

CHAPTER

2

The stallion strode into full view, standing tall and splendid in the yard. His blue-gray speckled coat and flowing black mane were even more striking than they had seemed in Jillian's dream.

"Oh, he's gorgeous," Jillian breathed. Smiling at the young stallion, she put her hand on Conall's neck, curling her fingers into his thick ruff.

But then Jillian got a look at the roan's expression—his ears were laid back flat against his head, and he danced on all fours as if the ground were burning his hooves. His eyes rolled and Jillian could see white around the rims.

"He seems upset," Conall commented.

At the sound of the wolf's voice, the roan shied, dancing sideways. Conall's neck ruff bristled, and he let out a low growl.

"It's all right," Jillian said, trying to calm them both. She held out a hand tentatively toward the horse. "No one's going to hurt you. What's your name?"

The stallion whinnied, and a dull gray cloud wisped like faint smoke off his body. The cloud expanded, floating toward Conall and Jillian.

"What is that?" Jillian cried in alarm.

"Get back," Conall growled, and leaped protectively in front of Jillian. He snarled a challenge to the horse.

The stallion reared up to his full height and boxed his front hooves in the air. Jillian clapped both hands to

her mouth. This meeting was not going well at all! Then the cloud reached Conall, and he started sneezing uncontrollably. He backed away, panting in ragged wheezes.

"What's wrong?" Jillian cried. "Conall, are you all right?"

Conall turned toward her, and Jillian saw that his eyes were red and watery. He flattened himself on the ground and covered his nose with his hooves. The cloud's odor, although weakening, was still strong enough when it reached Jillian to bring tears to her eyes. She recognized the scent instantly.

The speckled roan smelled overwhelmingly of pepper.

Luckily for her, Jillian didn't have a wolf's heightened senses. To her, the smell was pungent, but not unbearable. She sneezed once, which seemed to clear her nose.

The horse stomped his feet, flicking his tail, obviously agitated.

"He's afraid," Jillian said, but Conall just groaned in reply from where he was huddled. Jillian held out her arms, palms up, and stepped toward the horse slowly. "It's okay," she whispered.

The stallion stared at Jillian, breathing heavily, as she inched toward him. When she was a few feet away, Jillian stopped. "I'm glad you're here," she said. "What is your name?"

The horse released another cloud of pepper. Along with it, he sent an image of himself standing in a field of small, bushy trees covered with bunches of green, red, and black berries. Pepper plants! Jillian realized that the smell was her answer—Pepper was his name!

The image was tinged with such a strong sense of fear and anger that Jillian gasped. As she sucked in her breath, a wave of pepper hit her throat, making her cough and sneeze. Yes, the powerful cloud had been an answer to her question, but Jillian suspected that it was also meant to punish her and Conall. Why, she wasn't sure.

"What did I do to you?" Jillian choked out. "We just met . . . didn't we?"

Pepper bared his teeth at her and then rushed toward the beds of orange and white star-aster flower beds lining the wooden fence south of the cottage.

While Jillian wiped her stinging eyes, Conall wobbled over to stand beside her. He was still panting. "Not what you were expecting?" he growled.

"No," Jillian admitted. "He seems a bit . . . difficult."

"Difficult?" Conall replied with a barking laugh. "He's *awful*. He smells terrible and he's dangerous. You should just send him back to wherever he came from."

Jillian sighed. "I can only call animals—I can't send them away," she said. "And even if I could, Pepper appeared in my dream for a reason. And he's not rushing off, so perhaps he thinks he needs to be here, too."

Conall and Jillian turned when they heard Pepper whinny loudly from the flower bed. Jillian shook her head as Pepper began stomping the orange and white star asters, crushing them with his hooves.

Conall snorted. "Well, until he stops making that smell, I'm going to stay far away. I can't take it." He wobbled toward the brook as fast as he could on his horse legs.

Jillian stayed, staring at Pepper as the horse kept destroying the flowers. Despite his temper and strong smell, Jillian still felt a pull toward him. He seemed recognizable, as if she'd known him from somewhere before her dream. If only he would behave . . .

"Pepper, please stop smashing the star asters!" Jillian called out. "That isn't nice."

Pepper stopped and blinked at her. With a final back-leg kick, he launched the last patch of white star asters over the fence. Seeming satisfied, he shook his mane and ambled across the lawn, disappearing behind the side of the cottage.

Jillian bit her lip, wondering if she should follow him to the back garden. *Maybe I should let him be for now*, she thought. *Even though he doesn't seem to like me, I should give us both time to figure out why I dreamed about him and if we need to know each other for some reason.*

"Hello," said a deep voice behind her.

Jillian whirled around and saw Cade Traveler, the manager of the Trails End stables, standing shyly on the cottage path. By his side was Noble, his giant ambassador hound. "Oh, Cade!" Jillian exclaimed. "You startled me!"

Cade lowered his head. "I do apologize," he said anxiously. Even though Cade was a very well-respected man in Canter Hollow, Jillian felt touched by how nervous he always was around most people—he related much more easily to animals. "I . . . I just came by to check on Conall again, to see how he's doing with his shoes."

"Why don't you ask him yourself?" Jillian replied. "I'll call him." She closed her eyes and concentrated on her best friend. It took almost no time to make the connection and beckon him, since she'd basically been connected to Conall since he was a pup. Seconds later, Conall was trotting across the lawn.

Noble barked when he spotted Conall, and Conall howled happily. They rushed together and jumped around and rolled on the grass, playfully nipping at each other's heels. They'd been fast friends from the first time Cade had brought Noble for a visit. Cade let out a booming laugh when he saw his big, serious dog having such a great time with Conall. Jillian smiled, too—it was so cute seeing Conall behaving like a puppy.

After letting them play for a few minutes, Cade waved for Conall to come over. Conall wobbled to the stable manager, panting.

"How are the horseshoes treating you?" Cade asked.

Conall replied in his usual growl, and Cade glanced up at Jillian for a translation.

"He says they're fine for walking and running," Jillian repeated, "but he still misses his claws. He's frustrated by not being able to fight, dig, or run easily."

Cade nodded. "Can't say I know of any hoofed animal who can—"

The thudding of hooves interrupted Cade as Pepper trotted around the corner of the cottage.

"Hello, what's your name?" asked Cade. Before Jillian could answer, Cade strode toward the horse. Jillian hurried after Cade, but they both stopped when Pepper reared up and boxed his front legs dangerously. The roan released another odorous cloud and then bolted around the back of the cottage again.

"I should have warned you not to ask his name," Jillian said apologetically. "I don't know why that horse is so rude. But his name is Pepper."

Cade sneezed loudly. "Ah," he said, wiping his eyes. "Pepper, of course. I know most of the horses in Canter Hollow, but I don't recognize him. Where did he come from?"

"I dreamed about him," Jillian explained, "and so I called him. He showed up right away. He seems to have some sort of problem with me—actually, with everyone—but I think it's important he's here. I'm just not sure why yet."

"Well, that roan is a long way from home," Cade replied. "He looks like the Travelers' horses—blue roan tends to run in their bloodlines. He's got spirit, for sure. I knew only one other Traveler horse who was able to release smells, though."

Jillian's eyes opened wide. "You're a Traveler?" she asked. "Of course you are! Cade *Traveler*! I'm a Traveler, too . . . but I was taken away from my family as a baby. What are they like, the Travelers?"

"They're a mysterious folk," Cade replied. "They move around a lot, following their horses to the best grazing spots. They keep to themselves, though. I wish I could tell you more, but my parents came to Canter Hollow when I was young, and I haven't visited the Traveler camp since. They don't take kindly to outsiders, even ones born to their tribe."

That evening, Jillian couldn't stop thinking about the Travelers as she cooked dinner for herself. *I don't belong here, not really,* she thought. *I belong with my family. But will they accept me after I've been gone so long?*

Her thoughts were interrupted by a loud pounding on the outer wall of the cottage. Pepper was kicking the wall again, as he'd been doing all evening. It seemed as though he wanted her attention, but every time she'd gone outside to see him, the roan had just bolted away. Jillian wasn't about to go out and check on him again. "Quit it, Pepper!" she yelled.

His only response was an obnoxious neigh.

Jillian stirred a pot of soup hanging over the hearth, pushing Pepper out of her mind. She stared into the fire, wondering if her mother would even recognize her after so much time had passed. The fire blurred in her vision, and she had a strong flash of memory: a campfire flickering in the center of a circle of Travelers' wagons. Her father's laughter returned to her once more, and she saw her parents' yellow and turquoise caravan. Home.

Dropping her spoon, Jillian hurried to the door of the cottage and burst outside, calling for Conall with her ability. Her friend raced through the darkness to her side.

"What's the matter?" Conall growled. "Did that horse hurt you?"

"No, no," Jillian replied. "Conall, do you know where the Travelers are?"

Conall sat back on his haunches. "More or less," he answered. "They roam the lands near Styginmoor. We wolves often raided the Traveler camps. But those people move around, so they could be anywhere in a range of hundreds of miles."

"Could you lead us there?" Jillian asked.

Conall let out a long breath. "I know the general area," he replied. "But it would be very dangerous. What if Ivenna catches us near her realm?"

"It's worth the risk," Jillian decided. "I can't stand feeling homeless like this any longer. We're going, Conall. Tomorrow."

3

*E*arly the next morning, Jillian packed her few possessions and some supplies into a bag and headed to Canter Hollow with Conall. Before she left the cottage grounds, Jillian explained to Pepper where she and Conall were going. Pepper seemed agitated by the news, but then, Pepper seemed agitated by just about everything. Jillian tried to say good-bye, but the roan just turned his back on her.

Jillian still wasn't used to the bustling activity and noise of Canter

Hollow—she hadn't even seen another human besides Ivenna in all the years she lived at Styginmoor castle. She felt nervous walking into town, jumping at the calls of street vendors and flinching as horses thundered past.

Conall kept close to her side, eyeing the townspeople warily. "They're staring at me," he growled.

"You're unique, Conall," Jillian told him. "Be proud of it." But the stares made her feel more out of place than ever. She couldn't help worrying that Ivenna's curse on Conall had come true—that he would never be accepted anywhere, neither in the world of people and horses nor in the world of wolves.

When they reached the marble horse fountain in the center of town, Jillian turned south, toward the Trails End Stables on the banks of the Fastalon River.

The Stables was a vast complex of buildings, meant to house any horse visiting Trails End, as well as to provide a center for horse education, training, health, and breeding. Jillian and Conall found Cade training a group of foals in an enormous paddock.

Jillian leaned on the paddock fence as she watched Cade stretch out his arms and wave them up and down gently in front of the foals. She gasped in surprise as all the foals spread stubby wings and copied Cade's movements. These were air horses learning to fly!

When wing practice was over, Cade noticed Jillian and made his way over. "Hello," he greeted her. "Trouble with Conall's horseshoes? Or are you having problems with Pepper?"

"It is about Pepper," Jillian replied. "Conall and I are going to find the Travelers. I was hoping you could look after Pepper while we're gone. Maybe you could bring him to the Stables? I'd like to know someone's taking care of him—someone he could learn to trust. Maybe

he'll even tell you why he's here."

Cade blinked at her. "Hmm," he said. "Yes, of course I'll look after Pepper . . . but do you really think it's a good idea for you and Conall to travel to the other side of North of North? That sounds like a dangerous adventure."

"I'm going," Jillian said firmly. "I need to find my family. Conall will keep me safe."

"Just think it over," Cade suggested. "You'll be going through wild territory. The Travelers often camp near Styginmoor, which is guarded by—"

"I know!" Jillian interrupted. "I *grew up* in Styginmoor, remember? Conall and I fought beside Bella to free some magical friends from Ivenna and the wolves! Thank you for your concern, but I've made up my mind. I'm going to find my family."

Cade held up his hands in surrender. "As long as you know what you're getting into."

"I do," Jillian replied, her tone softening. "I'm sorry. Maybe Pepper's been rubbing off on me. But . . . I feel this *pull* toward the Travelers. Going there is the only way to find out who I really am."

"I understand," Cade said, nodding. "Well, come with me, then. I've got a few things to give you for your journey."

Feeling embarrassed that she'd snapped at Cade, Jillian quietly trailed after him with Conall close behind. They followed Cade up a flight of wooden stairs that led to a spacious loft. Conall had trouble stepping up the stairs, but he made it up with no grumbling.

Cade passed his office area—chairs, shelves, and a big wooden desk—and headed toward the back of the loft where storage crates were stacked. "Over here," he called.

Jillian helped Cade slide a heavy wooden trunk out of the stack. She stepped back as he opened it.

"These are keepsakes from my Traveler days," Cade explained. "Most of it is just sentimental childhood stuff, but there is one thing you may find useful—oh, here it is." He pulled out a dark brown cloak with a green hood and shook it free of dust. "It's a Traveler's cloak," he explained. "All our people wear them. This was my mother's."

Taking the cloak from Cade, Jillian tried it on. It fit perfectly, and was made of a soft, sturdy material that felt luxuriously warm. Jillian spun around, loving the way the cloak draped over her body.

"Thank you," she said. "I'm sorry I was rude before. It's just that this is so important to me."

Something heavy in one of the cloak's pockets bumped against Jillian's leg, and she reached down to locate it. The inside of the cloak was sewn with many hidden compartments, and so it took a second to find the lumpy object.

Finally, her hand closed around it, and she pulled it out.

It was a small leather bag, tied shut with straps. Jillian glanced up at Cade. "What's this?"

"Huh," Cade murmured, taking the bag. "I haven't seen one of those in years." He undid the straps and opened the satchel. A fresh scent of rich soil wafted out.

"That smells wonderful," Jillian said. "So natural."

"It's called Earth loam," Cade explained. "It's a magical mixture of things—the exact ingredients are kept secret by the Travelers. If you sprinkle it on any plant or seed, the loam will make it spring to full growth, including ripe fruit or vegetable. So as long as you have edible plants around, you'll always have a meal." He passed the bag back to Jillian. "Take it. Food isn't always easy to come by when you're traveling. But use it sparingly."

Jillian slipped the bag back into a cloak pocket. "Thanks again," she told Cade.

"You're welcome," Cade replied. "I still think it's dangerous, but I'm impressed that you're setting out on this quest. If I didn't love my work here so much, I might be tempted to go with you . . . to rediscover that old Traveler part of myself, too."

Jillian nodded and turned to go back downstairs and start her journey.

"Oh, wait!" Cade called out. "I almost forgot." He hurried over to his desk and grabbed a folded bundle of oil-cloth. "Conall, these are for you."

Conall sniffed the bundle, watching intently as Cade unwrapped it. Inside were four sets of sharp metal claws. Conall let out a low growl of amazement.

"I had Mr. Smithin, the black-smith, make these," Cade explained. "Look, they attach right to your shoes."

He kneeled down and bolted the claws onto Conall's hooves.

Conall stepped around the loft experimentally. He no longer wobbled as he walked, now that he could grip the ground. Conall bounded over to Cade and licked his cheek in gratitude.

Cade laughed. "All right, all right," he said. "Now you can really protect Jillian on this journey, hmm?"

Nodding vigorously, Conall caught up to Jillian on the stairs, where she ruffled the fur on his head. His climb down with his new claws was much easier than the climb up had been.

At the bottom of the stairs, Jillian froze. Standing in the wide stable doorway was Pepper, glaring at her.

"What does *he* want?" Conall growled.

"It's all right," Jillian told Pepper. "Cade will look after you while I'm gone."

A torrent of powerful images from the horse hit Jillian: Pepper alone at the cottage—abandoned, lonely, and angry because of it. Then he was walking alongside Jillian through the woods. They'd obviously been traveling a long way.

"You . . . you want to come with me?" Jillian asked in surprise.

Pepper stamped on the stable floor—a firm yes.

"No," Conall snarled. "No way. We can't have him stinking up our trip."

Cade stopped on the step behind Jillian. "Oh, Pepper's arrived already."

"He wants to come with me," Jillian explained. "But I don't think—"

She was interrupted by another vision from Pepper: a clear image of himself leading Jillian up a high, snowy mountain. As they reached the top, Jillian could see the Traveler camp spread out in the valley below. The Travelers' campfire glowed in welcome in the center of the circle of caravans.

"Oh!" Jillian said. "He knows how

to find the Travelers!"

"I know the way," Conall snarled. "We don't need him."

"No," Jillian told Conall gently, "you don't know the *whole* way. You can get us close, but you don't know how to find the camp. Pepper says he does."

"Riding Pepper would get you there much faster," Cade offered, over Conall's growls of protest.

Pepper neighed loudly, shaking his head. He sent an image to Jillian, *her walking behind him*, repeating it until she held up her hand for him to stop.

Jillian fixed her gaze on Pepper's eyes. "All right," she said. "Here's the deal. You can come with us—*if* you let me ride you."

Pepper threw a major tantrum—clopping his hooves, bucking, turning around in the doorway, whinnying loudly. Small trails of his pepper cloud wisped off his body.

"That's the deal," Jillian repeated.

"Take it or leave it."

Breathing heavily, Pepper faced Jillian. Then he lowered his head, his ears back flat. He'd take the deal, Jillian knew, but that didn't mean he had to like it. Apparently, though, he wanted to come with them badly enough to accept it.

Before Pepper changed his mind, Cade outfitted the horse with a halter with soft rope reins. Pepper absolutely refused a bit in his mouth—or a saddle, for that matter. Jillian hugged Cade and thanked him again.

"Come on, Conall!" Jillian exclaimed. "Let's find the Travelers!" Then she climbed onto Pepper, and they headed off on their quest.

"Good-bye, my friends!" Cade called after them. "And good luck!"

CHAPTER

4

Jillian rode Pepper at an easy pace westward, following Conall past Rolands Hold Arena, toward the smaller villages and farms of Trails End.

The weather was gorgeous, and the landscape around them was lovely, with well-tended fields and orchards sparkling in the sunlight. But Jillian didn't have much time to admire the dazzling scenery. She was too busy trying to keep herself safely mounted on Pepper.

The roan made riding him as difficult as he could. He would stop suddenly, almost pitching Jillian over his head into a bush, or speed up into a canter without warning. He skipped steps abruptly, jostling her, and tilted his body to either side, making her stomach lurch. As someone who had ridden a horse only once before—Bella, the great leader of all North of North horses, who moved with balletic grace—Jillian had to be constantly alert to Pepper's next trick.

Conall stayed far ahead on the trail, keeping away from the scent that made him sneeze. Any time Conall got too close, Pepper made his smell stronger. Pepper also reacted to Conall's closeness by sending out frantic images—shadowy creatures slinking around him—terrified memories that haunted Jillian's mind for hours afterward.

As night fell after their first day of traveling, Jillian was exhausted and lonely, having been unable to speak with Conall all day. A kindly farmer let them stay overnight in his barn, although

Conall slept outside.

The second and third days of travel were more of the same. The farms were getting farther apart as they gained more distance from Canter Hollow, and the villages were smaller, with occasional empty grassland on either side of the road and dark forests appearing on the horizons. To pass the time, Jillian tried to focus on her memories of her family, but it was difficult with Pepper's constant tilting, bucking, and random crowhopping.

By the time the sun went down on their third night, Jillian hadn't seen a farmhouse for hours, so she set up camp alongside a burbling stream. She made a fire with matches she found in another pocket of the Traveler's cloak, and ate a small dinner of bread and fruit while Pepper grazed nearby.

Conall hunkered down beside her. "I told you it was a bad idea to let him come with us," he growled.

Jillian sighed. "You may have been

right," she admitted in a whisper. "It's just that he wanted to come for some reason, and I do feel responsible for him, since I called him to me. Also, I just couldn't pass up the chance to ride. But now I'm feeling more tired than if I'd walked." She leaned her face against Conall's soft fur. "Will you stay close tonight?" she asked. "I've never slept outside before. It would be good to know you're nearby."

"I'll always guard you," Conall swore. "Always."

As the giant ringed planet rose beside the moons in the night sky, Jillian wrapped herself in her cloak and fell asleep, listening to Conall sneeze.

Jillian was awakened in the morning by Pepper blowing a raspberry in her face. "Ugh, Pepper," she groaned as she sat up. "Do you always have to be so horrible?"

Looking pleased with himself, Pepper went back to grazing.

Assuming Conall was out hunting

his breakfast, Jillian gathered her things and ate some fruit, waiting for him to return.

An hour later, Conall still hadn't come back, and Jillian was starting to get worried. "He's never stayed away this long," she told Pepper.

Pepper pricked up his ears and sent Jillian an image: Conall running away through fields, getting smaller and smaller as he disappeared into the distance.

"You mean he *left*?" Jillian cried. "For good?"

Pepper let out a nicker.

"I don't believe it," Jillian said.

But after another hour passed and Conall still hadn't returned, worry started to make her feel sick to her stomach. Finally, she decided to continue on the road they'd been traveling toward the border of Trails End, and hope Conall would meet them along the way. Jillian saddled up Pepper and rode him along the path, biting her lip as she scanned the horizon for any sign of her friend.

Conall wouldn't just leave me, she told herself. *He promised he'd always guard me. But he's never stayed away so long without telling me.*

Lost in thought, Jillian wasn't ready when Pepper suddenly stopped short and crowhopped. She slid off his back and landed on her rear end.

Scanning the path, Jillian saw a tomtomme bounding into the brush, its long tail waving behind it. *That* was what had spooked Pepper? A tiny mouse-like creature? "Ow! That was just plain mean!" she scolded the horse, as she climbed to her feet.

In reply, Pepper blew a raspberry.

With a long sigh, Jillian stood in the middle of the road, wondering what she should do. Without Conall, she could never find the way to where the Travelers roamed on the other side of North of North—Pepper knew only the last part

of the journey. Jillian knew she could call Conall with her ability and compel him to return to her, but she didn't want to force her friend to do anything he wasn't willing to do. He had to make up his own mind. She had almost resigned herself to turning back toward Canter Hollow when she heard a howl behind her.

"Conall!" Jillian hollered. "We're here!"

Conall came racing up the road—from the direction where they had camped for the night. He was panting when he reached Jillian's side. "Luckily . . . it's easy . . . to find you—I can smell . . . that horse from miles away. Why . . . why did you move? I told the horse to stay put while I went out scouting."

Jillian glanced at Pepper, who performed a jaunty little tap dance in the road. "Ugh," she replied, as she realized the truth. "He made it seem like you weren't coming back."

Conall bared his teeth at Pepper,

who bared his own right back. "And you believed him?" Conall asked Jillian.

"No!" Jillian replied. "But I didn't know where you were, so after a couple of hours, I figured we may as well continue the way we were going. I never doubted you—I was *worried*."

"I woke up early," Conall growled, "because I couldn't sleep from all the sneezing. So I went scouting around, looking for a faster way to travel. I told Pepper—"

"I get it," Jillian said. "We've got to watch out for that horse."

Conall grumbled grouchily. "You watch out for him," he snarled. "I've had it. I can't be near him—it's too irritating for my nose, like the worst sickness. I can't take it anymore."

"What do you mean?" Jillian asked. "You're not giving up on our quest?"

"No," Conall replied. "No, I promised I'd lead you there, and I will. But I'm going to keep scouting far ahead, and I'll leave marks for you to follow. I'll check back with you once or twice a day and guard you when you sleep, but otherwise, I'll be out of sight."

"If that's the way it has to be," Jillian said glumly.

"It is," Conall answered. And he loped away, racing down the road.

Irritated, Jillian climbed onto Pepper's back and grabbed his mane roughly with her hands. "Listen, you," she told the horse, "I don't know what your problem is, but I'm sick of your games. Now be good and let's just get to where we're going, okay?"

Pepper immediately tried to buck her off again, but Jillian held on tightly.

"I'm watching you," she said.

5

*B*y late afternoon, the road had turned into a dirt path that wound into a sparse forest. At the border of the woods, Jillian spotted a mark from Conall—a deep scratch on a tree at her eye level that he'd made with his metal claws. Seeing the scratch reassured Jillian that they were on the right track, but it also made her miss Conall terribly.

For the hundredth time since they'd left Canter Hollow, Jillian regretted her decision to let Pepper come along. She couldn't let this horse come between her and her best friend!

The shadows in the forest got longer as dusk settled in. They followed Conall's markings to a small, muddy glade, where the sound of night insects was rising in intensity as the sun set. Jillian wondered if the glade was a good spot to set up camp for the night, so she dismounted to check how wet the ground was.

A big swarm of bugs flashed all around her, rising from the mucky soil. "Oh, look," Jillian said. "Fireflies! Aren't they pretty?"

Pepper's hide twitched nervously. He flicked his tail at the flashing flies and produced a peppery cloud.

As soon as the cloud hit the flies, they buzzed wildly, their lights flashing brighter and faster. More rose up from all around the glade. They swarmed around Pepper and Jillian, dazzling them with flickering brilliance.

A fly lit briefly on Jillian's arm,

and she grabbed the spot in pain. "Ow! It *burned* me!" she cried. "These aren't fireflies! They're *flame* flies!"

The dangerous insects sparkled and shimmered around Pepper and Jillian. The air was so thick with the flashing bugs, and Jillian's eyes became so dazzled by their glare, that she lost track of which way she and the horse were turning.

Behind her, Pepper flinched as one of the flies burned him with its hot flash, and he released another cloud of dense pepper scent.

The flame flies buzzed into a frenzy again, singeing Pepper's mane and scorching Jillian's cheek. Pepper released another cloud in response to the attack.

"Stop!" Jillian cried. She waved away the brilliant flies, starting to sweat from all the bursts of heat exploding around her. "You've got to stop with the pepper cloud!" she yelled at him. "It's just making them crazy!"

As he got burned again, Pepper

whinnied in pain and stamped his hooves, radiating more of his strong aroma.

"If you don't stop, they're going to cook us!" Jillian screamed.

Pepper's eyes rolled in panic, and his smell got stronger yet.

As Jillian frantically patted out a spark in her red hair, she was struck with a sudden thought: *The more upset Pepper gets, the stronger his pepper smell becomes.* It seemed obvious now, but she'd never made the connection before.

She grabbed the sides of the horse's face and looked directly into his rolling eyes. "You've got to calm down," she told Pepper. "Control your emotions." *Or we'll never get out of here alive*, she almost added. But she kept that thought to herself, knowing that would only fuel his terror.

Pepper was puffing short breaths and stepping around frantically, his smell getting even stronger. Jillian wasn't even sure he had heard her.

The howl of a wolf cut across the glade. For a second, Jillian's heart leaped with hope. *Conall will save us!* she thought. But as he heard Conall's cry, Pepper started sending out panicked images—dark wolves attacking him—and his smell only got worse.

"Conall!" Jillian screamed. "Move away! You're scaring him!"

The wolf howl cut off, and Jillian desperately dug into the hidden pockets of her Traveler's cloak, hoping to find something that would calm the panicked horse. She found a small compass, a spool of string, . . . and then a big lump of brown sugar.

She popped the lump into Pepper's mouth and then cupped her hands on either side of his eyes like blinders, ignoring the painful burns the bugs flashed on her hands and Pepper's powerful odor. "Eat that," she whispered into his ear. "It will help."

As Pepper chewed, Jillian tried

to think of a song that would soothe him. She started humming, and it was only after a few moments of whispering the tune into his ear that she figured out what the song was. It was a melody her father had sung to her when she was going to sleep as an infant: a Traveler lullaby, almost forgotten in the far reaches of her memory.

As she hummed, Pepper stopped twitching so much. After a long moment, the intensity of his aroma faded, mixing with a faintly sweet smell. He was finally calming down. As Pepper relaxed, the flame flies began to calm, too, spreading farther away across the field.

The second Jillian could see the edge of the forest again, she scrambled onto Pepper's back, and rode him out of the glade into the cool darkness of the woods.

Jillian searched the dark forest for shelter and found a thick copse of trees near a short hill. As she and Pepper settled down, a faint rain began to drift from the sky. Luckily, the canopy of trees above her was so dense that it kept them dry.

Exhausted and stung by small burns all over, Jillian slumped against the trunk of a tree, fading toward sleep.

Before she drifted off, she spotted Conall up on the top of the nearby hill, silhouetted against the giant ringed planet in the night sky. His wet body shivered as he stood guard. Jillian had no doubt that she'd hurt his feelings by screaming at him when he was trying to rescue her, but there he was, still guarding her as he had promised.

Oh, Conall, she thought sadly. *Is finding my family worth all this difficulty? Is it worth being burned all over and sleeping in the rain? Is it worth this wedge that Pepper is driving between us?*

CHAPTER

6

During the next few days, Pepper didn't give Jillian any trouble as they followed Conall's markings through the hilly forest country of North of North.

Well, he didn't give any *active* trouble. Pepper had fallen into a sullen, depressed mood, which was almost as bothersome to Jillian as his nastiness had been. It was awful being around the morose horse—especially since the landscape they were traveling through was so incredibly splendid.

Growing up in dark, dismal Styginmoor, Jillian hadn't known how beautiful North of North truly was. When they crested one bare hilltop, she actually gasped aloud. A vast forest of pine trees was spread out below her. As Jillian watched, single trees in the forest shivered, and all their needles turned silver momentarily before returning to green, flashing in intricate patterns across the vista. With so many trees blinking randomly across the forest, it almost seemed as if the evergreens were communicating with one another in a complex language. Maybe they were!

Another time, they reached a clearing in the woods where a tall waterfall crashed down into a deep pool. Mists from the cascade floated up, swirling and tumbling in the air like watery, winged spirits, glistening against the leaves.

It was all so breathtaking—and Pepper didn't seem to care about any of it. Every time Jillian witnessed another beautiful sight, she wished Conall were by her side instead of scouting ahead. But instead she was stuck with this miserable horse, who didn't seem to care at all about the floating jackrabbits, moaning yellow mushrooms, or gravity-defying marble cliffs they'd passed on their journey.

Jillian followed Conall's markers, but saw her friend only briefly in the evening, when he circled back to guard her while she slept. He always stayed far enough away so that Pepper's smell didn't make him sneeze.

One night, in a densely wooded part of the forest, Jillian woke when she heard a strange scraping sound. She sat up and peered into the darkness. By the light of the moons, she watched in amazement as Conall leaped up onto the trunk of a wide, tall tree, clinging to the side with his metal claws. Hoof over hoof, he climbed slowly up the tree until he reached a high enough limb so he could get an overview of the surroundings.

Jillian curled sadly into her cloak, sorry that she hadn't seen Conall's tree-climbing practice during the previous days. He was using his new claws to do things no wolf had ever done. She was missing her friend's day-to-day triumphs, and she fell back asleep feeling very alone.

After more than a week of travel, the forest finally thinned out, and one morning, Pepper stepped past the tree line into a vast field of tall, golden grass.

Pepper stopped at the edge of the plain, prancing nervously, his ears flat against his head. Jillian sat up straight on his back—Pepper was more alert than he'd been in days.

"What is it?" Jillian asked.

With a low neigh, Pepper sent her an image: the shadow of a massive bird of prey swooping menacingly overhead. Jillian scanned the sky and even turned around to look up at the trees behind them, but she didn't see anything unusual.

"I think we're safe," Jillian told Pepper. "I don't see any giant birds. Let's keep going. Conall's last marker pointed us this way."

Pepper took a step backward, shaking his head.

"Come on, Pepper," Jillian urged him. "We can't turn back now—we have to cross the grasslands to get to the Travelers, don't we?"

Pepper backed up another step and flattened his ears, but then launched forward at a fast trot across the plain.

"Thank you, Pepper," Jillian said. "We'll be all right—you'll see."

On the last tree in the meadow, Conall had left a mark. It was an arrow pointing due west, and so Jillian lined up her compass to follow Conall's direction.

By mid-afternoon, all traces of the

forest behind them had disappeared, and around them was nothing but waving golden grass. Jillian pulled out her compass from her cloak pocket again to make sure they were headed due west. It would be easy to get lost in this endless plain, and with no more trees, Conall couldn't leave any more markers. Jillian hoped he'd find them again when night started to fall.

A dark shadow passed across the sun, and for a second, Jillian thought that rain was coming. It would be unpleasant to be caught in a storm with no shelter around.

But then Pepper whinnied in panic, and Jillian barely had time to clutch the reins before he leaped forward at a full gallop. She glanced back at the shadow.

It was following them.

She looked up to see a bird bigger than she'd ever imagined swooping down at them with its talons outstretched.

"Go faster!" Jillian hollered at Pepper.

Pepper needed no encouragement. In panic, he thundered across the plain.

Jillian looked up at the enormous bird again. It was nearly twice as big as Pepper, with dark orange feathers and a wingspan that almost blotted out the sun. Its gigantic beak was sharp, and each talon was as long as one of Jillian's arms. She recognized the bird as a roc, a legendary bird of prey—Jillian hadn't known they really existed. The roc screeched, chilling Jillian's blood.

On its next pass, the roc swooped down at them again, its talons missing Jillian's head only because Pepper swerved at the last second. Jillian flattened herself against Pepper's neck, silently urging him to gallop faster.

The next time the roc dived down toward them, Pepper released a dark cloud of aroma, which stunned the bird for a second. It sneezed and fell behind for a bit, but caught up again with a few beats of its colossal wings.

Jillian spotted a wide break in the grass ahead. She shouted a warning to Pepper, but her voice was lost in the wind of their rush and the screeching of the roc.

As the bird's shadow fell over them again, Jillian saw that the break in the grass was actually a deep ravine— and Pepper was barreling headlong toward it.

Jillian screamed as Pepper launched them over the chasm's edge. The roc's talons missed them by inches overhead as they toppled down the steep cliff.

They fell through the air at top speed, the valley below zooming toward them dizzily.

The wicked thorns in the valley below them glistened in the afternoon sun.

With the roc swooping after them, Pepper and Jillian hurtled down the cliff toward the briars below.

As they fell, Pepper's legs continued to gallop in midair. After a few strides, his hooves made contact with the sheer cliff wall, and he managed to steer toward a break in the briars. The small opening allowed them to pass through the tangled vines with only minor scratches. "Pepper, how did you do that?" Jillian gasped.

Overhead, the roc screeched in

frustration, unable to grab them with the brambles blocking its way.

Jillian was surprised to find that under the mesh of intertwined spiky vines was a shadowy hollow tall enough for her to remain on Pepper's back without hitting the thorns overhead. Thick stems jutted up from the ground, supporting the brambles above, but there was enough space to ride comfortably through the natural tunnels.

She was even more surprised to find that Pepper was calm in the vine pathways. He didn't hesitate in picking a direction to follow through the maze.

It was almost as if he'd been there before.

Looking around, Jillian noticed a woody-looking vine twining through the briars. On the ground were small, dried, wrinkled, black-colored berries.

When Pepper stopped to munch on a cone of green berries hanging from the woody vine, Jillian began to guess the startling truth.

The vine was a peppercorn vine. Jillian recognized it from Ivenna's herb garden. Ivenna loved spicy food.

Pepper was eating pepper berries!

"You *have* been here before," Jillian told Pepper. "When?"

After swallowing the berries he was chewing on, Pepper glanced back at Jillian, glared at her, and let out a snort. Then he returned to grazing on the pepper fruit.

"I will not drop the subject," Jillian replied. "You knew about the roc, and then you knew how to get away from it. You've obviously been in these tunnels before."

Pepper neighed loudly and danced, trying to jostle Jillian on his back.

But she didn't give up. "Tell me," she insisted. "Did you hide from the roc and live on peppercorns? Is that why you smell?"

Pepper reared up on his hind legs,

squealing in protest. Jillian ducked to avoid hitting the thorny ceiling and lost her balance, falling onto the ground with the dried pepper berries. She scooped up a few of the berries and stuck them into the cloak's pockets, thinking she'd grow them for Pepper when they reached the Travelers.

Wheeling around to face her, Pepper sent a torrent of images her way: himself as a skinny foal, wandering alone through a gray, rocky landscape. He was searching for something—or someone—but he'd gotten lost along the way. The young Pepper braved gusting snowstorms and sheltered himself from driving rain under rocky outcroppings, peering out at the foul weather with a lonely heart. He had no friends or family to care for him, and after a time he started to forget who he had been, forgetting what he still searched for, losing himself in the solitary wilderness. . . .

Jillian gently stroked Pepper's

nose, her heart going out to the forlorn foal. "Show me more," she urged softly.

She watched young Pepper enter the field of grass, and gasped as a roc chased him just as it had chased him and Jillian. Young Pepper had accidentally fallen into the chasm, although he'd gotten much more scratched up that first time.

He lived in the briars for longer than he knew, eating only peppercorns. The pepper kept him alive, and it also helped ward off the roc, who was always waiting above for any sign of the foal coming out—

A growl interrupted Pepper's story. Jillian peered around Pepper down the tunnel, hoping that Conall had found them.

But it wasn't Conall. Instead, a wolf almost as big as Pepper padded around a corner of brambles, glaring at Jillian with fierce black eyes. Another wolf followed the first, and they stood side by side in the tunnel, their jaws gaping open to reveal their sharp teeth.

Jillian backed up against Pepper's side, her heart thumping in her chest.

"It's the girl," one wolf snarled, recognizing her. "Jillian."

"Myrfor will be pleased," the other wolf growled.

Jillian felt a chill. These weren't just any wolves. They were warriors, sent by Myrfor, Ivenna's second-in-command and Conall's father. Myrfor's heart was as black as his fur. He frightened Jillian almost more than Ivenna did.

The wolves prowled closer.

Snorting, Pepper released a dense cloud of peppery stench.

The cloud hit the wolves right in their faces, and if Jillian had not been so scared, their reactions would have been funny. Their eyes rolled up in their heads, and they gasped for air before starting to sneeze and cough uncontrollably.

Pepper neighed, and Jillian leaped

onto his back. They fled in the opposite direction from the wolves, with Pepper taking the turns at breakneck speed.

"Those were Ivenna's wolves!" she yelled, as Pepper barreled through the maze. "This valley must be really close to Styginmoor! Get us out of here!"

Jillian glanced over her shoulder— there was no sign of the wolves, but they'd certainly chase after them as soon as they'd recovered.

Turning back around, Jillian ducked as Pepper burst from the briar hollow into the evening light of the valley.

A squawk blasted Jillian's ears. It was a good thing she was already ducking, because the waiting roc's talons missed her head by inches. The roc caught Pepper's shoulder with its wing, though, causing him to stumble sideways against the brambles. Jillian felt thorns stab her through her Traveler's cloak, and she arched her back against the pain.

Unable to keep her seat, she slid to the ground.

Pepper scrambled to his feet, and Jillian crawled closer to the briar to avoid being trampled by his hooves. Above her, Pepper pressed himself against the thorny vines, shielding her from the roc.

As the roc swooped down again, Jillian realized what Pepper was doing—the roc couldn't get close enough to grab them with the bramble bush extending above. The gargantuan bird screeched and flapped its wings in annoyance, sending dust swirling into Jillian's face.

A blood-curdling howl echoed down the valley, and Jillian almost burst into tears—how could they defend themselves against Ivenna's wolves when the roc would grab them if they moved?

But the howl hadn't come from inside the briar. It came from a dark wolflike creature leaping down the rocky cliff.

Conall!

Jillian jumped to her feet as Conall landed directly on the roc's back, piercing through the bird's feathers with his metal claws. Shrieking, the roc twisted in the air, trying to peck Conall off its back with its beak. But Conall dodged the snapping beak and gouged the bird with his sharp horseshoes. The roc squawked in pain.

She was so caught up in the battle that Jillian didn't notice Ivenna's wolves coming out of the briars until Pepper whinnied in alarm.

The stallion pushed in front of her, already releasing wisps of peppery cloud. The wolves backed off a little, wary of having their senses assaulted again.

Then the bigger wolf glanced over at the battle with the roc. His eyes narrowed as he recognized who was fighting the giant bird.

"Conall," he snarled. "The traitor."

"Kill Conall!" the other wolf howled. "Kill the traitor!"

The wolves started to slink toward the fierce battle.

"No!" Jillian yelled. Without a thought for her own safety, she jumped in front of the wolves. She pulled the bag of Earth loam from the pocket of her Traveler's cloak. "Move, Pepper!" she yelled, and tossed a handful of the loam at the thorny vines around the wolves.

The effect was quicker than she had dared hope. Pepper leaped out of the way just as the brambles burst into furious growth, thickening and sprouting in every direction. Vines looped around the wolves, lifting them off the ground. The wolves howled in pain, poked by hundreds of thorns, tangled in the densely intertwined briars.

"Serves you right!" Jillian shouted.

She turned around just in time to see the roc fling Conall off its back. Jillian gasped as Conall bounced off the cliff wall. He landed in front of the screeching bird.

The roc raised its head up, opening its beak to strike.

"Conall!" Jillian wailed.

Pepper leaped into the fray, landing right over Conall. The horse let loose with his darkest cloud of pepper odor, which went up the roc's open beak.

For a second, the roc froze in place. Then it gagged, fluttering its wings. Stumbling backward, it righted itself and flapped out of the valley, screeching and sneezing the whole way. Pepper whinnied in triumph.

Jillian heaved a huge sigh of relief. Behind her, the wolves whimpered, stuck in the briar patch. The battle was over—for now.

Under Pepper's sheltering form, Conall moaned in pain. Jillian rushed over and dropped to her knees beside her friend. Conall had a deep gouge in his side, with blood oozing into his fur.

He was badly hurt.

*P*epper nickered anxiously and sent an image to Jillian: the dark shadow of the roc gliding over-head.

"I know it'll come back," Jillian replied. "More wolves will probably come, too. We've got to get Conall out of here and stop his bleeding. Can you carry him?"

"I can walk," Conall growled. He struggled to sit upright, and then pushed himself painfully onto his hooves. He glanced over at Pepper and blinked, his eyes filled with surprise. "Let's go. Now."

As they headed out of the mouth of the valley, Jillian walked beside Conall. She could tell he was in pain with each step he took. Pepper stayed a little way behind, not wanting to cause Conall any more discomfort with his peppery smell.

Luckily, they reached a stand of purple baobab trees that gave them shelter before night fell—or the roc returned.

In the morning, Jillian pressed them to hurry onward, hoping that if they reached the Travelers quickly, they could heal Conall's wound. But the wound had stiffened after a night's rest, slowing them down even more.

For two days, the group straggled through marshy land in the direction of the Travelers. The landscape around them became harsher and less welcoming the closer they got to the outskirts of Styginmoor. The castle was on the far side of a vast swamp, and the smell of stagnant water and rotting soil was even stronger than Pepper's scent. Despite the fact that they were surrounded by water, most of it was too foul to drink.

Around sunset, they came across a pond fed by a fresh stream trickling out of the rocks. Conall collapsed on the mossy bank, so exhausted that he was barely able to lap water from the pond. Jillian bit her lip when she saw how weak he was—his wound must have been worse than he was admitting.

Jillian wished that Ivenna had let her learn from the master herbalist at Styginmoor, but she had been strictly forbidden to visit the apothecary. Still, the rose dragons and violet pixies around the castle had shown her a few things about herbal remedies. "Pepper," she called, "go see if you can find some twelve-leaf berries, but only the blue ones. They may help Conall."

Pepper neighed and trotted into a small patch of woods to search for herbs. Jillian allowed herself a small smile—defeating the wolves and chasing away the roc had definitely changed Pepper's attitude for the better!

Sitting beside Conall, Jillian scooped water into his muzzle. His breathing was ragged and shallow, and Jillian stroked his head, terribly worried about her friend.

A tiny noise caught Jillian's attention. She got up to investigate when she saw the flicker of a small tail in a hollow log.

When a little animal hopped onto the log, Jillian flinched, but then smiled when she got a good look at it. The furry creature blinked at Jillian with its bugged-out eyes. She couldn't identify it—it had the head, tail, and front paws of a squirrel, but its back legs were webbed and folded oddly underneath it, and its eyes bulged out on either side of its fuzzy face. Whatever it was, it was awfully cute.

"Hey, little fella," Jillian cooed at the creature. She pulled a lump of sugar out of her cloak and offered it to the animal.

Jillian's mouth dropped open in shock when a long tongue shot out of the creature's mouth and snagged the sugar lump. Then it jumped over to a bush, where it let out a croak.

Can it really be a squirrel . . . crossed with a frog? Jillian wondered. She didn't know such a combination was possible, but then, her best friend was a mixture of wolf and horse! *I'll call it a squog*, she decided. *Or is frirrel better? No, it's more of a squog.*

The bush rustled, and more creatures began to emerge. They sniffed the crumbs of the squog's sugar lump and headed Jillian's way. She thought she recognized a sloth blended with a squill ninny; a rabbit colored like a fuzzy wooble; a whiffle bear with deer legs; a pig mixed with a bubble turtle; and something larger and nervous that she couldn't immediately figure out with fur, stripes, big teeth, wings, a dorsal fin, and a fuzzy tail. *Maybe it's a chipmunk-bat-shark?* Jillian wondered. *A chipbark? Bashamunk? Shachibat?*

Jillian passed out chunks of sugar lumps to them all, and they gathered around her, squabbling over the bigger pieces. Despite her worry about Conall, Jillian giggled—they were all so adorable!

Pepper returned with a sprig of a green plant in his mouth. As he stared in amazement at the mixed-up creatures frolicking in the glade, Jillian took the plant from him and sniffed it. It was a particularly powerful shoot of mint.

Before Jillian could scold him for not bringing back something more useful for Conall, Pepper let out a cheerful whinny. A greenish cloud released from his body, and Jillian smelled a strange combination of the sweet mint and pepper. "Have you been eating this stuff?" she asked the giddy horse. "I think you've created peppermint!"

While Jillian was talking to Pepper, more combination creatures emerged from the woods, in a mixture and variety of species that amazed her. The ones she had given sugar made their way over to Conall, sniffing the suffering wolf-horse.

Jillian was about to tell them to leave him alone when she saw that they were applying soothing pond lily leaves to his wound. They obviously recognized Conall as one of their own. Conall moaned in relief as his pain eased.

Jillian's heart went out to the creatures. They, too, must have been transformed by Ivenna's terrible experiments. She watched in amazement as Conall's wound began to seal up from pond lily juice.

"Jillian," Conall growled. "It will

take me a few days to heal. We're close enough to the Travelers that Pepper can lead you from here. These animals will take care of me—and I want to spend time with them. They are . . . just like me."

"No," Jillian cried. "I can't leave you. I won't."

Conall let out a long sigh, his head drooping back onto the mossy bank.

Biting her lip, Jillian reconsidered what Conall had said. He did look exhausted and haggard, and the creatures were taking care of him. *And he needs to find some place he truly belongs as much as I do,* she realized. "Maybe you're right," she said.

"I am," Conall groaned. "Go."

But what if the roc finds him? Or Ivenna's wolves? Jillian worried. Then she had an idea about how to protect him until she returned.

Pulling out her bag of Earth loam, Jillian paced around the edge of the glade, sprinkling the precious dust. Wherever the loam landed, plants shot up taller than Pepper, making a dense hedge around the pond and Conall. She used up the last of her Earth loam, but it was worth it.

"That should keep you safe," Jillian told Conall. She kneeled down beside him. "I'll call you when I find my family," she promised.

Conall nodded. "Or if you're in trouble," he added groggily. Then he rested his head on the moss and fell into a deep sleep.

9

Jillian rode Pepper westward across a landscape that grew more desolate the closer they came to Styginmoor. Overhead, storm clouds flashed with lightning on the horizon.

The weather fit Jillian's mood. It made her feel physically ill to have returned to the lands where she had been enslaved as a child. Ivenna's evil presence seemed to ooze out of the atmosphere. But she also felt a rush of elation as they approached the Travelers—she could soon find out who she truly was.

Pepper kept up his fast pace all through the morning and into the afternoon, when they emerged from a valley and began climbing a deer path up the side of a mountain.

For the rest of the afternoon, Pepper followed the trail along switchbacks, across narrow ledges, and between loose boulders. It was already evening by the time they reached the tree line, where the tall plants stopped growing because of the altitude. Up ahead, a yellowish snowcap began.

"We should camp here," Jillian decided.

She didn't dare make a fire, afraid of signaling their location to Ivenna's scouting wolves, so she spent a chilly night wrapped in her cloak. As soon as the sun rose, she and Pepper pushed onward.

Crossing the snowcap was treacherous, but Pepper knew a gentler slope up to the top. When they reached the peak, Jillian stared down at the land on the other side of the mountain.

There was a grassy valley, spotted by sparse trees, fed by a stream that ran down from the mountain's melting snowcap. Near the stream were three connected circles of brightly colored wagons and caravans, all arranged around large central campfires. Just behind the makeshift village was a small farming field, which looked brown and abandoned, although there was a large black tent set up in the center of it.

Smoke billowed up from the campfires, and Jillian's stomach lurched—she'd carried the memory of those fires with her throughout her whole life. Being so close to the people of her tribe almost didn't feel real. She had longed for this day forever.

Pepper neighed once and then hurried down the mountainside as fast as he could.

They reached the Travelers' camp

just before noon. Jillian dismounted quickly and walked beside Pepper toward the nearest circle of caravans.

Nobody came forward to greet her. Jillian smiled at the Travelers wandering by, but none of them met her eyes. She knew it was unreasonable to expect her people to rush up to her with open arms, welcoming her back home, but at least they could notice that a stranger had arrived!

As she got closer to the central campfire, she noticed that it was weirdly silent in the camp—there was no bustle of work, nor conversation between friends, nor the laughing play of children.

A peppery cloud began to seep out of Pepper as the hushed surroundings made him nervous. Jillian stroked his side, calming him as best she could. She didn't feel so calm herself!

As they passed through the first circle of wagons into the second circle, a mountain of a man stepped out from behind a caravan, blocking their path. He was extremely hairy, with an overgrown beard and bristly, bulky forearms. "What do you want?" he growled.

Before Jillian could answer, two more men joined the first in front of her. They all crossed their arms and glared at her with black, angry eyes. Behind them, Traveler women and children scattered, running into their caravans and closing the doors behind them.

Jillian shrank back against Pepper. "I was searching for the Travelers," she said. "Am I . . . am I in the right place?"

"You're not wanted here," the biggest of the men growled. "Take your horse and go."

"Please," Jillian said, "I've come a long way. I'm looking for my family. . . ."

Jillian let her words trail off as she noticed something disturbing. Behind the men, there were no boot prints where they had walked. Instead, their feet had made thick paw marks in the dirt. The men began to sneeze as Pepper's odor fully hit them.

"All right, we'll go—" she began.

"Go where?" a familiar voice said behind her.

Jillian whirled around.

It was Ivenna.

Jillian's old mistress sat on the back of Myrfor, her wolf companion. She gave Jillian a cold, sneering smile.

With her knees wobbling, Jillian cowered against Pepper. All the fears built up from the years of being Ivenna's servant came flooding back. She turned around, planning to jump onto Pepper and flee the camp.

But what she saw froze her in place. The giant men grunted as their bodies changed, thick fur sprouting everywhere. They dropped to all fours, quickly changing back into the vicious wolves they really were. Before Jillian could move, the wolves had surrounded her and Pepper, blocking their escape.

Ivenna laughed coldly. "I should have known you would come here," she said. "As you can see, the Travelers are now under my control. I came for their Earth loam to enhance my herbal potions, but it turns out that these silly people have let their supply run out. But all is not lost." Ivenna smirked. "Even these fools can be useful when properly . . . motivated."

"What do you mean?" Jillian whispered. "What have you done?"

Ivenna stroked the matted fur on Myrfor's head. "Oh, I simply told these people that if I didn't get the Earth loam I needed, I would have my wolves kill them one by one . . . starting with their children." She gestured beyond the caravans toward the brown farming field. "I razed their little garden to show that I was serious. That's where I set up my tent. I adore the sensation of sleeping on scorched Earth."

"I see," Jillian said. Surprisingly, the smell of Pepper's scent started filling her with a courage she wouldn't have felt otherwise. As Ivenna spoke, Jillian racked her brain for any plan to escape . . . but nothing came to mind.

"You'll love this part," Ivenna continued. "Guess who volunteered to get a new supply of Earth loam? Your parents! They're the only couple in this pathetic settlement who didn't have children . . . and so they thought they had less to lose."

Her parents! "Where are they?" Jillian demanded. "Tell me!"

"Ooh, you've gotten bossy during your stay with the horses," Ivenna said mockingly. "It doesn't suit you."

"Where are my parents?" Jillian asked again.

Ivenna shrugged. "They went up that mountain," she replied, pointing to the snowy peak at the opposite end of the valley. "Apparently, there's a giant there who guards the loam. Your parents left weeks ago, though, so I suspect they're dead. Or they're just cowards who ran off and left their people to die."

"They wouldn't!" Jillian protested hotly. "They must be in trouble!"

"You think?" Ivenna drawled. "Why don't you go and find out, then?"

Jillian leaped onto Pepper's back. "I will," she retorted.

Ivenna clapped her hands. "Listen," she said, "if you or your parents don't return here with Earth loam in three days, I'll start feeding little Traveler girls to my wolves. I've already waited weeks, and my patience isn't limitless, you know."

In reply, Jillian and Pepper broke out of the ring of wolves, galloping through the camp and across the brown field toward the mountain.

As they raced away, Jillian tried to ignore the sound of Ivenna's evil laughter echoing in her ears.

CHAPTER

10

*E*ven with Pepper traveling his fast-est, it took most of the day for them to reach the mountain on the other side of the valley. Along the way, the ground sloped sharply upward, so by the time they entered the rocky foothills at the base of the mountain, they were already high enough for the ground to be icy.

The cold wind whipped at Jillian's red hair as they followed the trail up the flank of the mountain. She put up her hood to keep warm. The cave entrance was near the summit, and it took hours of walking over the snowy path to get to it.

Jillian dismounted beside the entrance, which was a smooth, wide hole leading into the depths of the mountain. "Pepper," Jillian whispered, "I think this tunnel is a lava tube. This isn't any ordinary mountain—it's a volcano. Let's hope it's inactive!"

After peeking around the corner to make sure the entrance was unguarded, Jillian and Pepper stepped inside. The tunnel's high ceiling was supported by twenty-foot-tall timbers that trembled as Jillian and Pepper walked past. Dirt and small stones tumbled from above with each step they took.

Jillian saw an orange glow at the end of the tunnel, which turned out to be the sunset reflecting off the snow coating the inside of the volcano's deep bowl of a crater. A steaming pool of sulfurous water bubbled in the middle, fogging up the view. Jillian thought she saw two people shuffling and hunching over by the edge of the pool, gathering something that they then dragged over to a small grayish pile with the help of two horses. She saw no sign of any giant.

"Maybe those people are my parents," Jillian whispered to Pepper, but they were too far away and the crater was too steamy to see clearly.

A wide path stretched from the tunnel down the slope of the caldera, but Jillian decided to wait for nightfall before heading down.

Right at dusk, Jillian saw movement on the far side of the bowl. She peered out from the tunnel, as the biggest man she'd ever seen emerged from a cave at the base of the caldera.

He was at least fifteen feet tall, with massive, muscular arms and shoulders, and he was coated head to toe with ice, which made him hard to see against the snow. The giant stomped toward the people working by the pool, raising a wicked-looking whip above his head.

He cracked the whip, and the people stopped working. They hurried over to a big cage not far from the pool and led the horses inside. The cage's bars were white—Jillian's eyes widened as she realized they were made of ice.

After locking the people and horses in the ice cage, the giant inspected the small pile of the stuff the workers had collected—Jillian assumed that it was Earth loam—and then retreated back into his cave.

Jillian waited a while longer to make sure the giant wasn't going to come out again. Then she whispered to Pepper, "Let's go."

They went cautiously down. The pool itself was rimmed by knotty, reddish plants that trailed tendrils into the hot yellow water. On some of the plants, clear crystals of various sizes had formed.

Jillian and Pepper sneaked past the

pile of collected material as they headed toward the cages. It wasn't Earth loam, as Jillian had expected—it was a heap of the larger crystals, which glistened dully in the light of the moons.

As they neared the cages, Jillian saw that the captives were silently watching them approach between the stout bars of ice. Like Jillian, the people were bundled up warmly in Traveler's cloaks with their hoods up. Pepper stayed a few paces back as Jillian stepped up to the prison.

"Foolish Traveler," the woman whispered, "have you come to make yourself a slave to the giant, too?"

"Ride out of here while you still can," the man urged. "Go."

"I came here to find you," Jillian said, as she pulled back her hood, revealing her red hair. "I traveled all this way to find my parents."

The man and women stared at Jillian in shock. Their expressions of

disbelief turned to joy and then sagged into fear.

"Jillian?" her mother said, choking back a quiet sob. She lowered her own hood, uncovering her own red hair, shot through with streaks of gray.

"Is that our little girl?" her father whispered. "Could it truly be?"

Jillian's mother reached her arms out between the bars, and Jillian grabbed them. Tears trailed down her cheeks, turning cold before they hit her lips.

"You must go," her mother insisted, tears streaming from her own eyes. "If the giant wakes, he'll enslave you to work here collecting Quick until you die."

"Quick?" Jillian asked.

"The crystals. Quick is the secret ingredient in Earth loam," her father explained. "We Travelers used to collect it here freely, until the giant took over the volcano."

"I'll get you out of here," Jillian promised.

"How?" her mother asked. "The giant keeps the key with him in his cave."

Jillian stared at the cage. "Are these bars pure ice?" she asked.

"Through and through," her father answered. "The giant uses magic to shape ice to his purposes."

"Then I have an idea," Jillian said. She closed her eyes and concentrated, seeking a connection across the miles of North of North. This time she knew she didn't need her memory journal—her need was too great, and there was no option of failure.

When she was done, Jillian opened her eyes. Pepper snuffled softly behind her, and Jillian gestured for him to come forward. "I want you to meet someone," she told her parents. "This is Pepper, my . . . my friend. He helped me find you."

Pepper nickered a quiet greeting.

His nicker was answered by the horses behind Jillian's parents, who pushed their way up to the bars. The mare was a beautiful tan with a black mane, and the stallion was a speckled roan that looked identical to Pepper, down to the pattern of his spots. There was no question that these were Pepper's sire and dam.

Pepper rubbed his nose against his parents' snouts in turn, greeting them silently and tenderly after years of separation.

Jillian gaped in astonishment. How did Pepper's parents come to be here with her own parents?

Before she could ask, Jillian heard a buzzing sound behind her. It grew rapidly louder. She glanced around and saw a dense swarm of flame flies swirling toward her. "Here they come," she said. "Mother, Father, take the horses to the back of the cage, please. This may be dangerous."

"No more dangerous than being a slave in a Quick mine," her father said.

When her parents and the horses were as far away from the bars as possible, and the bugs were flickering around the cage, Jillian put her hand on Pepper's flank. "Okay, Pepper," she said. "Do your stuff."

Pepper released a thick cloud of his peppery aroma against the icy bars of the cage, and then backed away.

The flame flies buzzed into action, frantically flashing intense bursts of heat around the bars. The bars began to melt, but Jillian had forgotten how loud the buzzing of the flame flies was. The sound echoed like a saw throughout the caldera.

Just as the bars broke away on the cage door, the giant appeared in the mouth of his cave, blinking groggily at the commotion. When he saw that his slaves were free, he bellowed and raised his whip.

"Run!" Jillian yelled at her parents. "Take the horses and ride out of here! *Now!*"

"What about you?" her mother demanded.

"Pepper and I will stall the giant," she said. "Now go!"

Before he climbed onto Pepper's sire, Jillian's father grabbed two heaping handfuls of Quick from the pile. Then Pepper's parents carried Jillian's parents toward the ramp to the upper cave at a full gallop.

Flicking his whip, the giant headed toward his escaping slaves, but Jillian had a plan. "Pepper!" she yelled. "Pepper him!"

Pepper raced in front of the giant, narrowly avoiding getting whipped. As he rushed by, Pepper released a cloud of his scent, which made the giant sneeze.

As Jillian had hoped, the flame flies noticed the new cloud of peppery odor. They buzzed directly at the giant, scorching him and melting the ice on his body.

The giant batted at the insects with his enormous hand, but Jillian and

Pepper were already barreling toward the ramp. Clearing the flame flies, the giant stomped after Pepper, quickly closing the distance with his vast stride.

Pepper carried Jillian as fast as he could up the path, and dodged another blow of the whip. At the top, Pepper lunged into the lava tube, zooming between the shaky supports.

The giant chased them into the tunnel, but he was slowed down by the narrower space, so that Pepper regained his lead.

Near the outside exit, Pepper stopped suddenly and sent an urgent image to Jillian: her dismounting and running out of the tunnel without him.

"No," Jillian insisted, but Pepper promptly bucked her off and shoved her with his head out of the tube. Then he raced back toward the giant.

"Pepper, no!" Jillian screamed, but her father grabbed her and held her firm before she could follow the horse.

Jillian watched as Pepper halted a few paces in front of the giant. He released another cloud of odor and then galloped toward the exit again.

When the giant hit the cloud of peppery smell, he gasped for breath. And then he let out a giant-sized sneeze.

The sneeze shook the walls of the tunnel. The rickety supports toppled, and the ceiling collapsed on top of the giant with a sickening crunch.

The entire tube filled with billowing dust, and Jillian lost sight of Pepper. Had he been caught in the crush?

For a long moment—too long—there was no sign of the young stallion. His dam whinnied miserably.

Jillian let out a sob. "Pepper!" she cried, and her father hugged her tight.

"There he is!" Jillian's mother shouted. "Look!"

Covered in dust, Pepper staggered out of the tunnel into Jillian's embrace.

CHAPTER 11

*A*s soon as it was first light, the two happily reunited families began the long and dangerous journey back down the valley toward the Travelers' settlement. On the way, they quickly stopped to gather natural ingredients, including peat and silver pinesap, and mixed a new batch of Earth loam for Ivenna.

As they got close to the caravans, Jillian saw that Ivenna was waiting for them with her four wolves by her black tent on the scorched farming field.

"Oh," Ivenna said, when they arrived in front of her. "You survived. Too bad—my wolves were looking forward to a delicious meal of Traveler children."

"Will you leave my people alone now?" Jillian demanded.

"It depends," Ivenna replied. "Did you bring the Earth loam from the giant?"

Jillian pulled a large bag free from where it had been hanging on Pepper's saddle. She opened the bag and showed Ivenna the loam they'd created.

"Wonderful," Ivenna said, her eyes gleaming with greed. "Myrfor, take it from them. Of course, I've never been one for keeping promises. You wolves will eat children today after all."

Jillian had been expecting something like this. Before Myrfor could move, she dumped the bag of Earth loam all over Ivenna. She reached into her pocket and tossed the peppercorn berries she'd collected onto the field, too.

The burned farmland all around Ivenna burst into unrestrained life as the Earth loam activated the crops she'd damaged. Tall corn stalks sprang up, and cucumber and pumpkin vines encircled her feet as they produced enormous vegetables that weighed her down. Juicy tomato plants shot up across the field, blocking the wolves from attacking, while bean tendrils and gigantic heads of lettuce sprouted in rows as big as hedges. The sorceress let out a shriek of rage.

But Jillian knew the growth wouldn't hold off Ivenna and her wolves for long. She searched for the woody pepper vines and plucked ripe peppercorns in bunches, which she fed quickly to Pepper and his sire. Then she stepped back and closed her eyes, using her ability to make a connection with the individual who had always been closest to her heart—Conall.

"Get them!" Ivenna shrieked to her wolves.

Myrfor and the other three wolves leaped over the colossal vegetables on the field, snarling at Jillian's and Pepper's families. But before they could attack, Pepper and his sire stepped forward. Both released dark clouds of pepper scent.

The wolves crumpled on the field, sneezing uncontrollably and panting for air.

Jillian knew that the pepper smell wouldn't stop them forever, but that wasn't the point. The point was to slow them down.

In a few moments, Jillian was very glad to hear a familiar howl from the Travelers' camp. "Conall!" she shouted, as her best friend galloped past the caravans. He'd brought reinforcements, too—all the mixed-up creatures hurried behind him, hopping, jumping, sliding, and scurrying toward the battle on the field.

Following Conall and the creatures

were the rest of the Travelers, who waved pitchforks and clubs in the air as they rushed to join the fight.

The blended animals made a bee-line for Ivenna, eager for revenge on the woman who had transformed them.

Ivenna screamed as she was knocked down by the creatures, who swarmed all over her.

"Take her!" Conall growled. "Drag her away, to a place so far that she'll never find her way back!"

And the animals did just that, hauling Ivenna kicking, screaming, and cursing toward the mountain to the south.

Myrfor and the wolves gathered in a tight pack, snarling at their attackers, still coughing and blinking madly. But when they saw Ivenna being dragged away and the armed Travelers approaching, they quickly turned tail and loped off the field as fast as they could.

With Ivenna and the wolves gone,

everyone let out a cheer that roared across the valley.

Jillian grabbed Conall in a tight hug. "I'm so glad you're well again," she cried. "Thank you for coming to help."

"Did you doubt I would?" Conall replied. "I told you I would always guard you, no matter what."

Jillian hugged him again, but then looked up when he stiffened in her arms.

Pepper was standing behind her, gazing down at Conall.

Conall gently pulled free from Jillian and returned Pepper's stare. "I never thanked you," he growled at the horse, "for saving my life from the roc."

With a pleased whinny, Pepper nuzzled the top of Conall's head, and Conall licked him on the nose.

Jillian put an arm around each of her friends. "Come on, Conall," she said happily. "I want you to meet my parents!"

* * *

That night, the Travelers threw a feast to celebrate their freedom and Jillian's return. With the most bountiful harvest the valley had ever seen blooming in their garden, they could stuff themselves silly and still have enough food to carry with them on their travels in the coming year.

During the party, Jillian couldn't stop grinning as all the Travelers came up and congratulated her and thanked her for what she had done for their settlement, welcoming her back to their society with open arms.

They sat at a small table in front of their yellow and turquoise caravan, sharing bowls of deliciously seasoned vegetable dishes.

"I always knew this day would come," Jillian's mother said. "No matter how difficult it became to believe, I never gave up hope that I would see you again."

Jillian smiled at her mother. "I

dreamed about you every night," she told her mother.

"I was remembering," her mother began, "when you were a baby, how you loved to play with Pepper. The two of you were inseparable, always—"

"Wait," Jillian said. "I played with *Pepper*? We knew each other?"

"Oh, yes," her father replied. "I thought you knew. He was born only a few days after you were, and we'd never seen a horse and girl bond so early."

"We were so proud," her mother added. "He was a special horse, with the rarest of abilities, to smell like whatever he ate, just like his sire."

Jillian nodded her head. "Whatever he ate," she repeated.

Her father patted her arm. "When Ivenna took you, we all searched for months, but Pepper took it the hardest," he explained. "He went out looking for you and never returned."

Jillian sat for a long moment,

staring at her parents in amazement. "I was bonded to him as a baby," she said softly. She stood up suddenly. "Excuse me, but I have to find him right now."

"Go," her mother said. "We'll be here when you get back."

Jillian rushed toward the campfire, where Pepper was standing at the edge of the firelight with his parents and a few other horses. "Pepper!" she called. "We knew each other! We've always known each other!"

He neighed loudly and cantered to her side.

"I knew you were familiar to me," she breathed, stroking his arched neck. She even loved the faint pepper smell that lingered around him.

Then Pepper sent her a vision: As a heartbroken foal, he wandered, searching for her, feeling her pull even when she was locked away in Styginmoor. For weeks that turned into months and stretched into years, he stood vigil on the outskirts of Ivenna's land. He couldn't leave, because he knew Jillian was inside the castle. But the wolves wouldn't let him approach, no matter how tirelessly he tried.

The wolves finally chased him away, and Pepper rambled across North of North, lonely and afraid. He learned to use his anger to protect himself. He was lost to his friend, lost to the world he knew, and after being trapped in the bramble for months by the roc, finally lost to himself and his memories. . . .

The vision broke off, and Jillian hugged her horse tighter around his strong neck. "We've finally come together," she whispered to him. "We're together again with our families and each other. And now we'll always be together."

Pepper nickered as he nuzzled the top of Jillian's head.

They stood together, watching the

celebration around the campfire. Jillian laughed when Conall strode in, wiggling to the music. The mixed-up animals danced around him, gazing up at him with pure admiration. He had become a king to a misfit army of half creatures, and Jillian couldn't be happier for her friend.

The three of them—Jillian, Conall, and Pepper—had all found somewhere they truly belonged.

Jillian stepped over to a table heaped with all kinds of delicious fruits. "Pepper, come here," she said. "My father said you can smell like whatever you eat."

Pepper moved closer and nodded in agreement.

"So," Jillian said with a smile, "have you ever tasted a strawberry?"

Go to
www.bellasara.com
and enter the webcode below.
Enjoy!

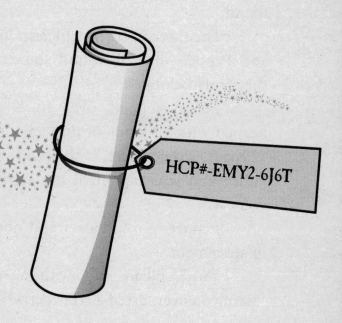

HCP#-EMY2-6J6T